THE LAND OF LONG AGO

AN *Elsa Beskow* BOOK

Floris Books

eep in the woods lay an old fallen-down tree trunk. It was covered in moss and its roots stuck out like legs. It looked like a dragon from a fairy tale.

Two children, Kai and Kelly, lived in the cottage nearby. They often played on the tree trunk, and in their games it became all kinds of wonderful things. Sometimes it was a horse, sometimes a dragon and sometimes even a crocodile.

One day, the children were in the woodshed looking for a stick to use as a riding crop, when they found a broken umbrella. They decided it would make perfect wings for their dragon, and they fastened it to the old tree trunk. It made him look real. They ran back to the cottage to look for a bridle and reins, so they could fly their dragon.

In a hollow oak tree nearby lived a mischievous gnome, who liked to play tricks on people — even though he was hundreds of years old. When the children went into the cottage, he sprinkled a magic potion over the tree trunk and it came to life!

Kai and Kelly soon came back out with a rope for the bridle. They sat on the tree trunk and shouted, "Fly out into the world, dragon!"

The tree trunk began to creak and groan, then it rose up into the air, grunting and growling. The children held on tight so they didn't fall off, and the dragon asked them, "Where shall we go?"

Kelly was too scared to make a sound, but Kai said, "To the Land of Long Ago please!"

The dragon spun round, sending moss flying everywhere, and flew towards the sea. And far beyond the sea lay the Land of Long Ago.

Kai, Kelly and their old tree dragon flew over the ocean for a long time, until they reached a small island. The children were tired, so they stopped to rest. They clambered off the dragon's back and wandered along the shore.

They soon came to a meadow, where a princess sat crying.

"Why are you crying, princess?" asked Kai.

"I'm all alone," sobbed the princess, "and my knight is locked in that tower over there."

"How can we set him free?" said Kelly, but the princess shook her head.

"The iron door is shut tight with huge locks."

"Who's got the key?" asked Kai.

"The king of the trolls," replied the princess. "He lives over on the other island with his flock of sheep. But quick, run away. Here comes the dragon who's guarding me."

A terrifying dragon with sharp teeth and claws rushed towards them.

Kai and Kelly ran back to their own dragon, who flew quickly into the air.

The wicked dragon hissed and leaped, but he had no wings to fly.

The old tree dragon laughed and flew down low over his head.

But Kelly wanted to help the poor princess. "Let's fly to the other shore," she said, "to find the king of the trolls."

They flew over the sea to the other island. Kai and Kelly climbed off the dragon's back once more and headed off to find the king of the trolls.

They knocked at a big wooden door.

"Who's knocking at my door?" thundered the king of the trolls.

"Just two shepherds who would like to herd your sheep," said the children.

The door opened and the king of the trolls looked out.

"You are very small shepherds," he grumbled. "You're no use for herding my sheep."

"Yes we are!" answered Kelly. "We've herded our father's sheep for two years."

"Well," mumbled the troll, scratching his head, "I suppose I could give you a try. My old sheep dog needs a rest. But if you lose just one of my sheep, you'll be in trouble."

The old sheep dog was very happy to get some help. He lay down and slept all day while Kai and Kelly looked after the sheep.

They were very careful not to lose a single sheep. But how were they going to get the key to the tower and rescue the knight?

One evening Kelly was singing a song to the smallest lamb.

"Sleep my lamb with your soft, white wool.
The sun is shining bright and clear,
The grass is growing fresh and green,
Making food for my little lamb.
Sleep my lamb with your soft, white wool."

When Kelly looked up, she saw the king of the trolls staring at her.

"What are you singing?" he asked. "Sing that song again." So Kelly sang the song again.

"You will sing that song for me while I fall asleep," said the troll.

"I can't do that," said Kelly. "The song is only meant for sweet little lambs."

"If I act like a sweet little lamb, then you can sing the song for me," said the troll.

"If you give me the key to the tower where you've locked up the poor knight, then I might sing the song for you," said Kelly.

The troll scratched his head, thinking. Then he pulled out a big key from his pocket.

"All right then. But now you must sing to me, like you did with the little lamb," said the king of the trolls.

Kelly promised that she would, and the troll lay down in the grass with the big key next to him on the ground.

Kelly sang her song again and again, and the troll grunted happily.

As Kai guided the sheep back towards their shed, he couldn't help but laugh at Kelly sitting there, singing her pretty song — "Sleep my little lamb with your soft white wool" — to the big, ugly troll.

The king of the trolls fell fast asleep, and he snored so loudly that you could hear it from far away.

Slowly and gently Kelly took the key and ran with Kai to the shore to wake their dragon. They flew to other island and clambered up the hill in the moonlight to the knight's tower. They unlocked the heavy door and freed the knight from his dark prison. He was very happy to be free at last.

When they woke the princess and she saw her knight, she laughed and cried with joy. Then they crept very quietly past the sleeping dragon guard.

But just as they reached their old tree dragon, the wicked dragon woke up. He clawed at the poor old tree trunk and snapped off some of its roots. The knight pulled out his long sword and cut off the wicked dragon's head with a single blow. Then they set off to the princess's land.

The sun was rising as they reached the princess's land, and her palace glistened like gold. She was very happy to be home again.

When they reached the shore, the old tree dragon lay down to rest. He had carried a heavy load and flown a very long way — much further than it looks in these pictures. And he had been badly injured in the fight with the dragon. So Kai, Kelly, the princess and the knight walked without him up to the great palace.

The people were overjoyed to see their princess return. They gathered around to wave and cheer. Blaring trumpets spread the good news throughout the kingdom.

When they saw their daughter home at last, the king and queen ordered a great feast. Kai and Kelly were given the finest clothes, and wore crowns on their heads.

It was agreed that the princess would marry the knight. The king had hoped she would marry a prince, but this knight was brave — he had slain a dragon — so the king was happy. Kai and Kelly walked down the aisle behind the bride and groom, holding the long train of the wedding dress. The wedding celebrations lasted for seven whole weeks.

Despite all the fun they were having, the children were starting to feel quite homesick. When the celebrations were over, they agreed to ask their friend the old tree dragon to take them home.

As the royal couple sailed off on their honeymoon the children headed down to the shore to find their dragon.

But while they'd been enjoying themselves up at the palace, the old tree dragon had been lying in the hot sun and he'd begun to rot. All the children found on the beach was a pile of broken wood.

"What can we do?" they sobbed. "How will we get home?"

The king and the queen comforted them and let them stay in the palace. They gave them lots of presents and let them play in the royal gardens all day long. But the children weren't really happy because they wanted to go home.

Outside the palace gardens was an enchanted forest, and one day the children saw some troll children staring through the golden gates. They looked so lonely that Kelly invited them into the royal gardens. She shared her toys and cared for them, and Kai played soldiers with them.

But when the king and queen came by, they were angry to find strangers in the palace gardens. The king chased the trolls out and locked the gates firmly behind them. He sent Kai and Kelly away to school to learn proper lessons like a real prince and princess.

But school in the Land of Long Ago wasn't much fun. They weren't allowed to go to the same school, and there were no other children to play with.

Kai had to read big, heavy books and learn to write difficult letters. The ink always made big splodges when he wrote, and the monks were very strict.

Kelly learned to read, and learned to sew with gold thread. But the thread always got tied in knots, which made the nuns unhappy.

One night, as dawn was breaking and Kai lay awake thinking of home, he saw a little gnome climbing through his window.

It was the gnome from the hollow oak tree at home! When the gnome saw how much Kai and Kelly's parents missed them, he felt bad about the trick he'd played and he set out to look for the children. He was so happy to finally find them, and he signalled for Kai to follow him out through the window.

 uch letters as this
Kai learned to write

And who was waiting outside? There was Kelly, sitting on the old tree dragon, who was alive again! The dragon was so happy to see Kai that he leaped around like a puppy.

The troll children had shown the gnome where Kai and Kelly were. They had gathered together all the pieces of the old tree trunk, and the gnome had sprinkled magic potion over them to bring the old tree dragon to life once more.

Normally troll children don't like humans, but they liked Kai and Kelly who had been so kind to them, and they gathered around them now and cheered.

And so Kai, Kelly, the gnome and the tree dragon set out on their long journey home. As they flew over the king of the trolls' island, the noise of the dragon's wings woke him up. He sat up, confused — Kelly's lullaby had sent him to sleep for all that time!

The old tree dragon flew faster and faster, until at last the children saw the forest and their little cottage. Their parents were outside raking hay when they heard a loud noise in the sky. They looked up to see Kai and Kelly flying through the air wearing gold crowns on their heads. You can imagine how happy they were!

While they hugged their children, the little gnome hurried back to his hollow oak tree before anyone could blame him for his little prank.

The old tree dragon threw off the torn shreds of his umbrella wings, and lay down comfortably in his old spot. No one would ever make him fly again. He closed his eyes and fell asleep.

Kai and Kelly didn't jump and ride on him any more. They knew that he needed to rest. They patted him gently and said, "Thank you for our adventure and for bringing us home."

First published in Swedish as *Resan Till Landet Längesen* by Albert Bonniers, Stockholm in 1923
First published in English by Floris Books, Edinburgh in 2010. Published by agreement with Rabén & Sjögren Agency
Text and Illustrations © 1923 Elsa Beskow. English version © 2010 Floris Books. Fifth printing 2021
All rights reserved. No part of this book may be reproduced without the prior permission of Floris Books, Edinburgh
www.florisbooks.co.uk British Library CIP Data available ISBN 978-086315-771-4. Printed in Latvia

Floris Books supports sustainable forest management by printing this book on materials made from wood that comes from responsible sources and reclaimed material